D1068296

And in the beginning. . .

And in the Beginning....

By SHERON WILLIAMS

Illustrated by ROBERT ROTH

ATHENEUM • 1992 • NEW YORK
MAXWELL MACMILLAN CANADA
Toronto
Maxwell Macmillan International
New York Oxford Singapore Sydney

Atheneum
Macmillan Publishing Company
866 Third Avenue
New York, NY 10022

Maxwell Macmillan Canada, Inc.
1200 Eglinton Avenue East
Suite 200
Don Mills, Ontario M3C 3N1

Macmillan Publishing Company
is part of the Maxwell Communication
Group of Companies.

First edition

Printed in Hong Kong by South China Printing Company
(1988) Ltd.

1 2 3 4 5 6 7 8 9 10

LIBRARY OF CONGRESS CATALOGING-IN-PUBLICATION DATA

Williams, Sheron.
    And in the beginning/Sheron Williams.—1st ed.
        p.   cm.
    Summary: Describes how Mahtmi created the first man from the dark rich earth of Mount Kilimanjaro and gave him a gift marking him as special.
    ISBN 0-689-31650-X
    [1. Folklore—Africa. 2. Creation—Folklore.] I. Title.
PZ8.1.M878 An 1991
398.2'096—dc20   90-43094

To grandma Lucretia,
who forever sees the beauty
of the darker hues

S.W.

To Cheryl

R.R.

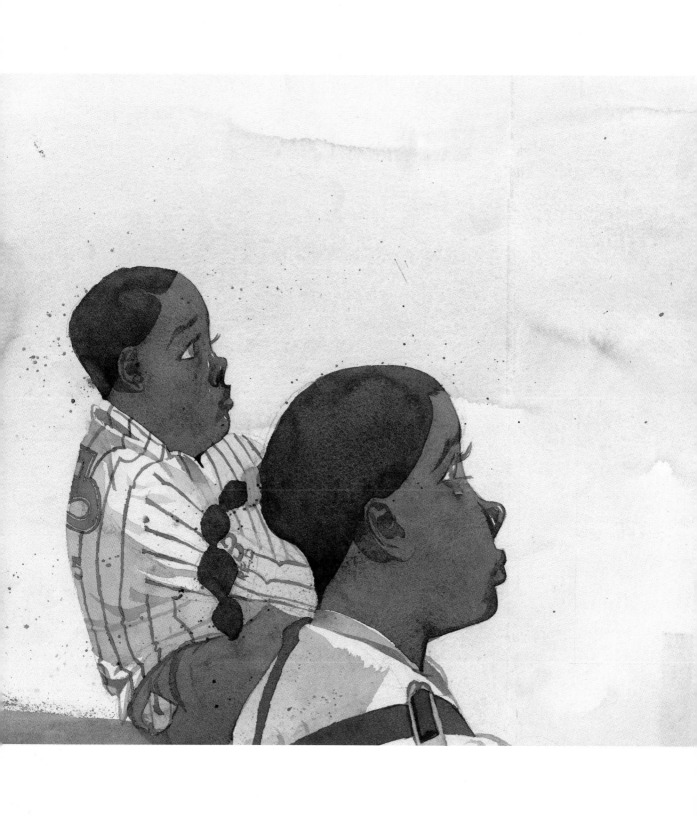

Shammama, my grandmother, tall and thin, reminded those who knew her of a pecan tree. Though she was very tall, she stood in a way that made her seem snarled. This was probably because she spent almost all of her adolescent and adult life bent over washtubs. Her skin was a warm shade of toffee beige, and her long bushy hair was roof-tar black. Strands of pencil-gray hair framed her face; her features were pointed and angular. Yet somehow the lines of her face came together to create a pleasant smile and the true beauty reserved for those people who do not regret a single thing about their lives.

While she was alive she showered us with abundant, unconditional love, and in her passing she left memories of strength, laughter, the world's best sweet-potato pie, and stories, stories, stories.

She conjured up tales filled with the imagery of black kings and queens, of lands where black people ruled in fairness and by divine right. She could always make the image ring so true, so alive. Her characters always approached life the way we children approached life: cautiously, yet with an all-consuming passion once we got ahold of it.

Shammama would sit before us gnarled around her favorite sitting stool, clasp her hands together, and always begin the tales with the ritualistic admonishment for purity:

Let those who would hear these words, hear. Let those that would seek to understand, understand. But to those who would change the moral of this tale, let them dwell in a place reserved for those who would not hear or understand, where they will not be heard or understood.

And in the beginning. . .

…Long before the world was separated into continents or countries by rolling sea tides or jagged mountains, Mahtmi, the Blessed One, began about his work of creating the original beings who would inhabit the world. This was a mind-provokin' task 'cause such a task had not been done before and 'cause he was eager to show the divine servants (some would call them angels) what one could do if one set one's mind to a thing. Had he not created the world on a short deadline of five days?

Still, there weren't no blueprints or guidelines to go by. What should "people" look like? Totally perplexed, he decided to go to the seashore, still steamy from its creation, to think on the divine matter for a divine while.

While he rested near the crystal blue waters and waded into their warmth, he pondered on the possibilities for mankind. Having no limitations can be a blessing in many ways and a curse in some others, Mahtmi thought. Should the outer covering resemble the blue waters of the seas or the warm tones of the sand? That fur concept he had reserved for the "bear" animal was nice. Yes, people could look any some kind of way…and it was a decision that rested with him.

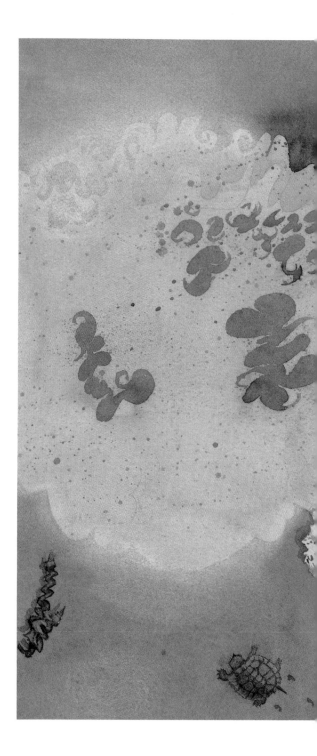

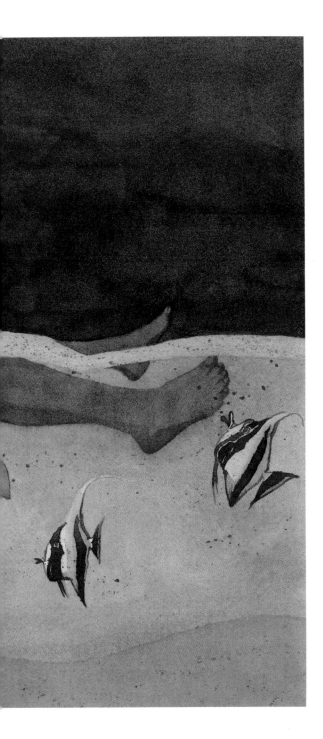

Mahtmi floated on the cresty waves of water and looked out into the blankness of the sky. Lost in thought, he began to doodle in its darkness with his forefinger as he considered the matter. Below Mahtmi's feet a small fish nipped at his toe. Mahtmi smiled with pleasure; even the smallest of my creatures seeks my approval and attention, he thought.

Mahtmi reached down lovingly to brush the creature aside and looked down into the crystal waters...and what should he see peering back at him but his own face, in a state of acute puzzlement.

"Why, yes!" he said. "People should look like me. I'll make a note of that."

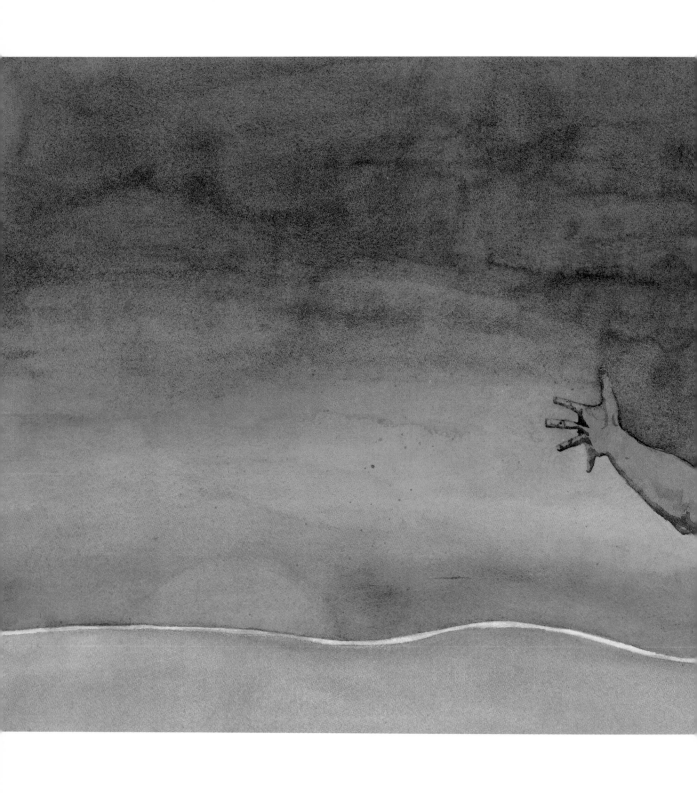

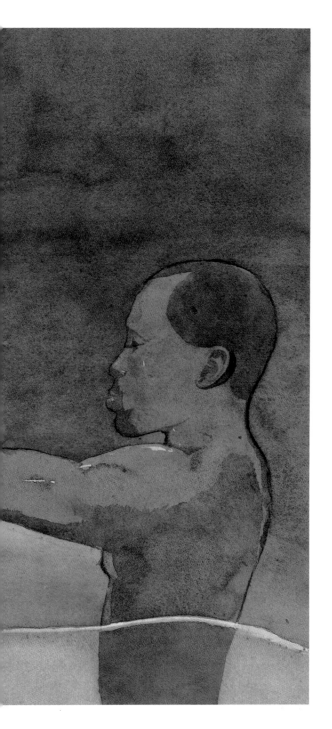

From the tip of his finger flowed vibrant hues and colors. Sunshine oranges and blood reds along with hints of evergreen greens and midnight blues pulsed out into the night and took up residence in the empty sky. He thrust a forefinger upward and what we now know as a sunset was fixed in the evening sky. They were merely the doodles of Mahtmi drawn on a thought-provokin' night, there to remind him of how he would make mankind.

On the morning of mankind's creation, Mahtmi rose early, searching the world for the materials with which to make people. When the beings and objects already in the world heard of the plans, they all wanted to give something to such a worthy cause. Mahtmi was pleased. He went to the foothills of the mountain we now know as Kilimanjaro, and the earth gave him its richest, darkest soil. The animals grazing near him presented him with their most durable hair and the "deer" animal offered Mahtmi his eyes, which Mahtmi took but replaced with a pair even more luxuriously brown. He went to the riverbed and spoke to the oysters on the matter of creating mankind. They made, each one, pearls so smooth and white that Mahtmi decided they should go in the very middle of the smile of people.

Laden with all the gifts from the beings of the world, Mahtmi began to create.

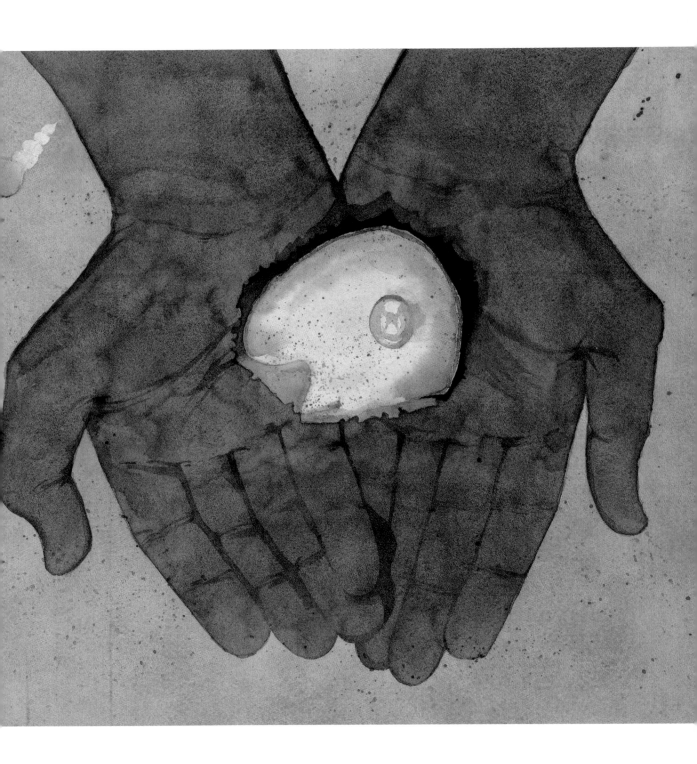

Under his hands the black soil waxed smooth, and as he fashioned the legs and arms they began to move under his touch. After the body was fashioned and the eyes and teeth were set in place, Mahtmi stood the being before him, gazed into the soft brown eyes, and placed a forefinger on this person's brow. He began to speak.

Wouldn't you know it, childrun? Mahtmi gave all of mankind the gift of thought and speech all with a single touch.

"The world is wonderful, Mahtmi…. Surely you should be praised for such a feat." The talk went on and on after that fashion for a long while. Must be a lot to say when you ain't never said nothing before.

Well, Mahtmi didn't interrupt at all and he didn't mind one bit. Intelligent company at last, he thought. He named that original being Kwanza, which in Swahili means, "the first one."

After a spell Kwanza grew accustomed to the beings and the bit of earth on which he had been created. He grew tired of the same sights, sounds, and smells. He envied Mahtmi when he came back from surveying the world to tell of this animal he had created or the other valley he had forged. Kwanza wanted to see some of these sights for hisself. Well, Mahtmi could sense that envy and didn't like it one bit, and after a thorough talking to Kwanza on the evils of it (that was the first sermon), he decided that perhaps Kwanza should go and view a little of the world for hisself.

Like any parent, Mahtmi wasn't really at all sure Kwanza was ready, so there were conditions. Kwanza would be allowed to see the world, but he had to check in every night. They decided to think hard on each other every night at just about the time Kwanza was getting sleepy, to send their thoughts to each other, so they could stay in touch and know if either needed the other. (And that was the first prayer.)

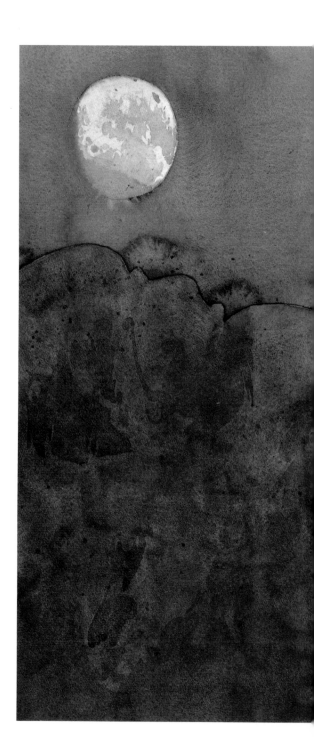

So it went that way for a spell, Kwanza sending his thoughts and Mahtmi getting them, Mahtmi sending his thoughts and Kwanza getting them. Now, you know, childrun, it just were not the same as being together. If you'd ever been alone, and I mean really alone, like Mahtmi was before he created the original one, you would kinda know and be able to understand how he felt. You don't know there is a crack in your heart till you feel the blood. Mahtmi had known loneliness before and didn't like its return at all.

Now, Kwanza weren't crying no river, mind you, but he was missing Mahtmi the same way; but you know how when you're out and about seeing new sights and smelling new smells, you kind of put that loneliness out of your mind. Well, that was the way with Kwanza. He was just so busy running about naming things and trying new fruits and such that he just didn't give Mahtmi the attention he should.

Like any parent, Mahtmi knew Kwanza would grow tired of being out and about in the world and eventually return home. Patience is the first virtue Mahtmi created, that's why he's as patient as they come. But he weren't no idler by no means, and he had a lot of time on his divine hands. So while he waited on Kwanza's return, he began to go about the earth expanding and experimenting on the world's configuration. Sprucing things up a bit—a waterfall here, a stripe on a zebra there—like a new bride getting things situated.

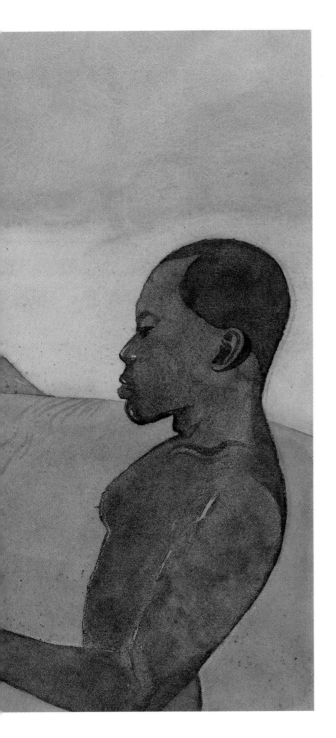

After a spell he began to experiment with his finest creation, humankind. He created another being out of the red soil of what we now know as Georgia, another out of the sandy beaches of Normandy…another with horsehair for its head…fish eyes for this one's eyes, and on and on after that fashion, biding his time till the original one came home. For changes or no, Mahtmi doted on this original one as being the finest creature 'cause he had created him first and was fond of him in a special way.

In the meanwhile Kwanza was doing just what Mahtmi knew he was gonna do—new shoes is only new whilst they got their squeak. He was tired of new fruit, new animals and new places—they had done lost their squeak. He began to think hard on home. He missed the comfort he felt just being in the presence of Mahtmi and decided to send him that thought that very evening.

Well, Mahtmi heard that message and said to him, "Don't wait until morning. Come now. I'll hold the evening sky back for you till you arrive."

You see, just like your parents, he worried about Kwanza travelin' round at night— only him being who he is, he could do more'n keep a light on in the front room. So Kwanza made it up in his mind to do just what Mahtmi had told him to.

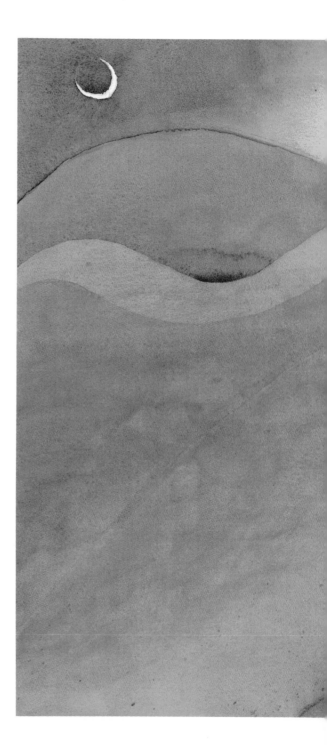

And when he arrived, what a ruckus he found. The sky was a-lit up every which a-way and stars was a-shooting from one end to the other. The birds was a-singing, 'cause that's what they prone to do. The beasts was a-romping, 'cause that's what they like to do. And the legions of divine servants was raising heaven (hell weren't created yet), 'cause that's what they bound to do. All in his honor. (And that was the first party.)

Well, he was so caught up in the goings-on that at first he didn't notice all the other manner of women and men that was around him. They was there, though—basking all about Mahtmi, being near him, and enjoying the comfort the original man had been missing.

Mahtmi welcomed him home and asked him, "How you like this party I done threw you?" And "How was your trip?" and all manner of conversation such as that.

But Kwanza began to notice other people about, doing this for Mahtmi and doing that…and wouldn't you know it, the brother to envy began to raise his little ugly head. Kwanza was jealous. Well, Mahtmi, being who Mahtmi is, sensed that rascal right away and pulled Kwanza to the side.

"Just what's wrong with you?" he asked. "These here is your sisters and brothers I created whilst you was gone exploring. That don't take nothing away from you."

Kwanza began to cry, for Mahtmi had never spoken to him in that way before.

Moved by his tears, Mahtmi asked, "Kwanza, why are you crying?"

"Well," he said, "they all looks better than me....This one here got red skin and that one's hair is so long and this one's eyes..." and on and on and on he went.

"What's wrong with your hair and your eyes and your skin?" Mahtmi asked. "Aren't they beautiful, too?"

"Well, after a fashion, I suppose," Kwanza said. "But my nose is so wide," he said.

"The better to smell the scents I gave every being and object," said Mahtmi.

"But my eyes is so big," he said.

"'Cause I wanted you to see everything," said Mahtmi.

"But my hair is just so plain," said Kwanza. "There ain't nothing special about me."

Well, Mahtmi thought on the matter for a spell and said to the man, "Don't cry anymore. Come to me at dawn and I will give you something special."

For you see, Mahtmi understands our needs even when we ain't got a firm grip on them in our own minds. He knew Kwanza wasn't really unsatisfied with hisself, he just wanted a little attention, a little sign that he was still very special to Mahtmi.

When the dawn arrived, Mahtmi sent for Kwanza and all of his sisters and brothers and all manner of creatures to come to the edge of what we now calls "Old Faithful." And he began to heat up the tips of his fingers in the fiery hot mist. Well, Kwanza couldn't imagine what he was gonna do with all that there heat. (He had done already created the world.)

Well, Mahtmi beckoned Kwanza to him and spoke to every creature in its own tongue and said

This is the original man, who I fashioned after my own image. I chose the black earth of Kilimanjaro to form his flesh—and the glistening of his skin is second only to my own. I chose perfect pearls for his teeth, and his smile delights me with its brilliance. I fashioned his mouth wide and full to taste everything good the earth can offer. He is beautiful, if you believe I am beautiful. From this day forth I will set him apart from every other man forever.

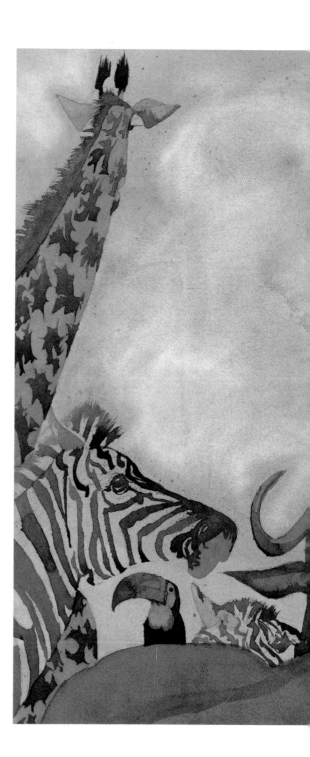

And with that said, he brought Kwanza to
him and set him between his feet and with
his divine fingers tightly curled every strand
of hair on his head. Mahtmi, master of
everything, was also a master curler. That is
why to this day every daughter and son of
the generations of the original man has a
crown of curled hair. Because of the love
token given to them by Mahtmi.

Sheron Williams writes:

I am and always will be Clara Mae and Butchie's oldest girl—
the skinny one who loved to read by flashlight under the covers
long after the word was given to go to bed. I spent most of the
childhood I hold close and precious in a little town called
Hampton, Virginia, in the Chesapeake Bay area. There I was
surrounded by loving cousins, disciplined uncles, persistent
aunts, and great-aunts and great-uncles wise beyond their years.
There also was my maternal grandmother, Lucretia, the foun-
dation for many of my stories.

I was brought north to Chicago to live with my parents and
grew up on the South Side. I went into the military after high
school, and after I was discharged I returned to the Illinois/
Indiana area to go to college. I received a B.A. in theater and
sociology from Indiana University and I am completing my
graduate thesis in media communications at Governors State
University in University Park, Illinois. My family and I call Park
Forest, Illinois, home, and I am employed as an associate editor
by a reference publication house.

Robert Roth is a professional illustrator who lives and works
on Long Island, New York. He studied illustration at the
Rhode Island School of Design, where he received his B.F.A.
degree. He has been drawing since he could grasp a pencil and
can be seen almost any day carrying a sketchbook. In his spare
time he often draws from life, away from the studio, in order to
keep his eye alert. Roth's watercolors are held in private
collections and have been displayed in New York City.

And in the beginning… is set in 12-point Galliard. The display type is Architectura. The artwork is rendered in watercolors on cold-press watercolor paper and was color-separated by laser scanner.